AF433803

ENSNARED BY THE WEREWOLF

LILLIAN LARK

Ensnared by the Werewolf

Editor: Ellie, My Brother's Editor
Proofreader: Rosa Sharon, My Brother's Editor
Cover Artist: Lillian Lark

Content Warnings

* * *

Dear reader,
Ensnared by the Werewolf includes Chasing, sex with a
monster, knotting, rejected mate, babies, breeding, and a
tiny bit of non-consensual oral.
Be kind to yourselves,
L. Lark

* * *

For those who enjoy a chase.

CHAPTER 1
ℭBELINDA

This was a stupid idea.

I jolt at the hoot of an owl and shake my head
in dismay. My days of being afraid of the dark are
long past, and as a witch, I'm more than capable of
handling anything I encounter in this forest, but
it doesn't stop the dark shadows being cast by my
cheerful light spell from being *spooky.*

The texture of the air seems to thicken and the
glow of the ball of light I'd summoned as soon
as I made it far enough from the nature reserve
parking lot wavers. The light the spell provides me
to navigate the floor of undergrowth and branches
softens. The shadows around me take on a fuzzy
look. Not the cute fuzzy, but the kind in a horror
movie when the director doesn't want you to know
what the ominous shape on screen is.

*Is an actual fog rolling in? All the gods above and
below, if the shadows start looking like creepy hands, I'm
going back.*

It had been the height of stupidity to trek into
the woods without contacting my date, but when I'd

parked earlier, the last rays of the day had lit the sky, and the forest appeared positively charming. The vibrations of the protection wards over the woods had been clear, and I'd assumed it would be easy enough to trace those sensations to the male creature I'm meeting with tonight.

A walk through the trees had sounded so *nice*, such a departure from being cooped up in my apartment, wallowing in heartbreak. I'd momentarily forgotten that I'm not what anyone would call outdoorsy. This was supposed to be a simple little hike to get to what would hopefully be a sexfest.

A walk would give me time to mentally prepare myself for the whole rigamarole of dating, even if this date is under strange conditions.

That had all been before the sun had set. Now, a lonely walk through the woods is inspiring the hair on my arms to rise and every sound has me swearing.

And I may be lost. The vibrations had seemed so clear from the outside of the woods, but it's as if the strands of magic are coming from every direction now and I'm starting to question my senses.

I should have just stuck to the plan. Get to the nature reserve parking lot, call my date to tell him that I'd arrived, he would have come to meet me, walking me to his cabin, and if all went well, we'd spend days fucking through his heat.

A guy going through *heat*. I've experienced my fair share of paranormal beings, but this is a first.

Just what I need to get my mind off a certain wolf shifter. To stop myself from making yet another useless phone call that he won't pick up.

When the matchmaker at the sexy bathhouse I used to frequent called me, it had seemed like deliverance.

Rose's voice had broken me out of my grieving state and provided direction. I just need to keep moving… and move on.

I don't know much about my date but had been given more details than usual because of the situation. This is an emergency match because somewhere in these woods is a being of some water variety preparing to go into heat.

Rose had made sure to express that while she believed that my mystery date and I were compatible, we aren't a complete match.

Not like a fated mate. I shake the thought and the pang it delivers away.

I am moving forward. Action over inaction.

So, I'd pulled on some fancy underwear, put in some contacts, thrown on a dress, and prepared myself to get fucked. I hadn't had the heart to put on one of my fancier dresses, my embroidery projects, though the dress with little skulls around the collar would have certainly matched my mood.

The one concession I'd made of my favorite art form for this date is my fabric headband.

I'd finished the moonlit forest design with a carefully stitched lone wolf howling right before my heart had been shattered. I wear it now as if it's a final goodbye.

This is me letting go.

At the very least, if I like this man, I'll be getting a good and thorough fucking. And maybe if things go well, we can talk about the future. It's not out of the realm of possibility that this guy could even convince me to carry his eggs. Stranger things have happened in this world.

Maybe this is exactly where I'm meant to be. The thought dispels some of the creepiness of my surroundings and leaves a pleasant tingle of truth down my spine.

And none of that will happen if I don't find that stupid cabin.

I pull out my phone again to check for service, to no avail. I sigh. Stupid magic in the air is probably scrambling my reception. If I make it out of this alive, I'll have to spring for one of those magically enhanced phones.

I could make my way back to the parking lot... I think. The floor of the forest is dry, and it's a struggle to make out the trail I've taken. My other option is to continue forward and hope to stumble over my date's place.

I rub my chest and the tingling from before seems to spread until goose bumps break out over my skin. I inhale air that is suddenly still. The sounds that I'd cursed for startling me are gone. There are no more owl hoots and distant crickets. The forest has fallen silent.

I swallow. Fear has my heartbeat starting to thud in my ears. The sensation creeping up my spine clicks.

I'm being watched.

I force myself to start walking deeper into the woods, trying to plan. Spells come to mind only to be dismissed.

My craft is more useful in deliberate slow projects, not combat. I can, theoretically, throw a stun spell, but it would require absolute focus. What could possibly be watching me? Or is it a who?

My steps start to quicken without me meaning to. Think, think, think. If it's a cougar or a bear, I can probably throw a stun spell.

A twig snaps, the sound reaching me over the rushing of blood in my ears. I stop and look back, scanning the foliage. The glossy leaves and craggy bark around me reflect the light from my spell. I don't see anything. And worse, the woods fall silent again.

The information comes rapid fire to my mind. Something is hunting me.

Something smart.

"H-hello?" I force out.

There isn't a response, but my raging senses know there's something there.

As my mind races, the light of my spell blinks a few times before sputtering out and the darkness envelops me.

I run.

A howl cuts through the night.

CHAPTER 2
JACK
ONE MONTH AGO

I stuff my phone in my pocket and huff. This is the place. The shop fits in with the bohemian café, multiple bookstores, and retailers with window signs proclaiming local goods on this street. There isn't even a glamour to disguise the true nature of this place. The words Stitching Magic are painted pristinely on the store window, overlaying a display of book stacks and crystals.

I wipe my hands on my pants and try to calm my nerves. No matter how many magic practitioners I visit, the nerves are always there. They even seem to get worse. As if every failed attempt to solve my issue chips away at the person I thought I was until I'm no more than a hollow statue of who I used to be before this affliction.

As if my hope dies a little each time.

The zing of otherness that runs over my skin is one more chip.

I can't keep doing this. I can't. Each time I meet with a new person, they do their best to help me, but ultimately fail and give me the information of another person to send me to. It's exhausting. I'm exhausted.

But there's still enough of the old self in me that rebels at the idea of giving up. A spark on the edge of being smothered.

Or maybe all this is useless and I should adapt to this new life. Give up all hope of solving this. I'm tired enough that the option offers relief, however hollow.

Something surges in my chest, and I grit my teeth.

Hunt!

The part of me that refuses to be silenced or tempered intrudes in my thoughts, breaking all attempts at introspection.

Find! Need! I want to snarl but push down the response. My inner beast is so much harder to suppress than before everything went to shit. I'm imbalanced, and the idea of staying like this has me moving to the entrance of the shop.

This is the last time. I'll give up after this time. I don't have the funds to keep doing this, but I can handle one last hurrah to try and end the struggle once and for all.

The bells are loud above my head as I walk in and freeze.

A goddess stands behind the front desk.

CHAPTER 3
BELINDA

I jump at the sound of the bell above the shop door, almost dropping my current embroidery project. The dreams from last night have left me a little on edge. Dreams of running through trees with an impossible mix of emotions: fear, adrenaline, and a tantalizing thrill that bordered on the sensual. I'd woken panting and confused.

I blow out a breath, trying to slow the race of my heart. I center myself before greeting the newcomer to my shop by finishing pulling the pale thread that will make up the moon of my thread nature scene. I love stitching nature because I can chaotically continue to add layers and details until my heart sighs with happiness.

The stranger fidgets in the entryway.

Finally calm, I blink at the man. The wards pulse at his presence, telling me that this isn't some human walking in from the street to ooh and ahh at my wares or to ask about casting a love spell. I've become rather jaded to humans pulling my magic shop up on Google out of curiosity.

Maybe I should take my cousin up on her offer for a ward to dissuade humans from entering the shop proper, but the situation doesn't seem to occur enough to make the time worth it.

It just makes me a little cranky.

But the man in the doorway isn't human and won't be asking whether the crystals on display would make good table centerpieces. Instead, this individual is wearing a glamour. I raise a brow at the visitor and carefully set my embroidery hoop next to the register. The man's dark hair is disheveled, and his hands are deep in the pockets of his jacket as if trying to make himself seem smaller. His face is attractive enough, but the appearance he's wearing isn't real.

Even still, his presence... *pulls* at me. Something in me perks up. What has fate brought me this day?

"Hello," I say. "What can I do for you?"

The man pulls his gaze from a framed embroidered design declaring *Get Witchy!* to me, and I suck in a breath. His eyes are a hazel so light that they almost look gold, and my body freezes for a moment as if I'm a rabbit halting in the presence of a hawk. No, that's not right.

A deer in the presence of a... wolf.

Ah.

The man's gaze drops, and he clears his throat. The spell over me that most certainly isn't magical in origin breaks.

The stranger looks around the shelves of spell books and lore encyclopedias.

"There are no humans here," I say. *We're alone.* I don't say that. It would be silly to go out of my way to tell a stranger that I'm all alone. Though... there's an odd feeling in the air that makes me think that I don't need to worry.

It's not that he feels *safe*. A shiver runs over my skin and my whole body is alight, alive.

Why do I trust him?

"I heard—" He cuts off before starting again. The man's voice is deep and smooth even if he seems to bleed discomfort. "I heard that you could help me."

Now it's not just my body responding to my mystery visitor. My professional interest rises, and I catalog the appearance of his glamour. His jeans are worn light in spots with what looks like sawdust brushed on one pant leg and the dark jacket is similar. The clothing he wears seems much too large for his frame.

I push my glasses up my nose. His glamour is a high-grade one that doesn't include the clothes he's wearing, so I'd guess this is a permanent glamour for him.

I let myself analyze just a small bit of the magic of the spell. The glamour is very well made from the tight stitches of power.

What is he hiding?

"That depends," I say. "What are you looking for?"

"I-I'm pretty sure I'm cursed."

CHAPTER 4
BELINDA

I bite back my excitement long enough to flip the open sign to closed and lock the shop door. Curses do not come along every day. My greatest skill and interest is in breaking curses, but the rarity of them means that a different source of income is necessary, hence the shop.

I do love my shop, but the idea of detangling some nefarious magic has me practically skipping.

The man freezes at the door of my workroom as if he's stuck in glue, and I mentally sigh at myself for forgetting.

"You need to remove the glamour before you can enter my domain," I say.

Distress flickers over the man's face and he looks like he's going to turn tail and run.

"I'd rather keep the glamour on," he finally responds.

I wince in sympathy. "This is a sensitive area. I can't have foreign magics working here."

"It's not pretty," he says. "I don't want to scare you."

I fold my arms. "I've seen a lot of ugly curses in my time."

Boils, rashes, speaking in tongues, hair loss, etc. The variety of curses never ceases to surprise me since the spells used for good are not nearly as diverse.

"The other curse breakers you've visited didn't require you to remove the glamour?" I ask.

"They were all able to work around it," he says before his eyes widen. "Not that there's anything wrong with you not being able to do that."

I wave a hand as if to brush away the comment. Everyone works in different ways. He looks around.

"Can you maybe turn around?" he asks. "Or turn off the lights?"

I take in the room, sympathetic to his discomfort. If I were to pull the curtains and click on the reading lamp, it would give him a semblance of privacy and allow me to still work.

Turn off the lights and sit in the partial darkness with a stranger. It's a terrible idea, but the feeling in the air is still there, tickling over my senses that it's important that this man is here. That he won't hurt me. But still...

"My name is Belinda," I say. "I'd rather not be complete strangers if I'm going to be alone in the dark with you."

And I just told him we're alone. Oh, well.

The man's smile is small. "I'm Jack."

With introductions handled, I move to darken the room. While I pull the curtains, the sensation of the atmosphere finally clicks. *The knowing.* I can count on one hand how many times fate has communicated to me via the instinct that all witches have, and it's never whispered quite like this.

I click on the reading lamp and aim it away before I lift a chin to the light switch next to Jack. He smiles at me gratefully before clicking the switch off. I try not to look at the silhouette of Jack in the light from the doorway while he moves, probably removing whatever object his glamour is embedded in. The shadow on the floor grows in size. The sound of stretching fabric and popping stitches is quiet but echoes in my brain. I only have time to blink before Jack closes the door and plunges the room into partial darkness.

I gesture to the chair across from me. "Why don't you start from the beginning?"

The chair creaks. "I don't know exactly where to start. It's not a story or anything."

I smile at the dark and try to keep from focusing on any details. "Whichever way you want to tell me. Why do you think you're cursed?"

"I'm stuck."

"Stuck?"

"Between forms, or something like it. I'm a wolf shifter and a year ago, I was shifting back into a human, and something strange happened. It was like it stopped. I couldn't shift at all. I can't go back to being all wolf, and my wolf form won't release me to be human."

I frown. That doesn't sound like a usual curse. No being forced to speak in riddles or being turned into a frog, just the halting of a natural process. I ponder that as Jack continues.

"The alpha of the pack I was associated with didn't know what to do with me, so I moved around, visiting different magic users until I ended up here."

"Your pack kicked you out?" I ask. That sounds very unlike the packs I'd come in contact with. Family is always first and foremost for every wolf shifter I've met.

"They didn't kick me out. I didn't fit in with that pack before this happened and after..." There's a rustle of movement as if the creature in the shadows is shrugging.

"Were there specific people you didn't get along with?" I ask.

"No," Jack says slowly. He sighs. "I wasn't raised in a pack. My mom is human and didn't know my father wasn't until I started sprouting fur and a tail."

"Oh." That's all I can think to say. I wince. "And he didn't stick around?"

"Maybe he would have," Jack says. "The local pack found me during my first shift and said they'd had a loner passing through that was killed by poachers at about that time."

"That's... incredibly unfortunate. I'm so sorry."

Jack's laugh sounds humorless and rough with an underlying growl to it. "Bad luck seems to follow me."

A shape moves in the shadows, a hand is splayed out as if to say *what can you do?* The fingers are much longer than a human's and sharp claws catch the light before he pulls them back.

I clear my throat. "Well, let's see what we can do about that."

I ask more questions, trying to pinpoint what's been dismissed by past professionals. I delve into all the details. The curse happened on Jack's twenty-fifth birthday. Many of the common avenues of curses have already been explored by other professionals, and one of them said the magic had a taste of fae to it.

I want to groan at that. Fae magics are not easily undone.

"May I touch you?" I ask. "I need to use my magic senses to see what we're dealing with."

There's a pause. Jack swallows. "Yeah. I guess you'd need to."

I wince in sympathy. "I can reach out my hands, and you can direct them since I can't see as well as I'm sure you do in the dark."

I stand and walk into the dark part of the room, lifting my hands out.

There's another pause before rough hands take my slender fingers. I hold in my gasp at the contact.

A connection lights at the touch, sending sparks of sensation through my very soul.

Oh. *Oh.*

Soul mate. I want to laugh in incredulity and then cry tears of happiness. Never in a million years would I think that I'd even have a soul mate, let alone meet them. I want to run my hands through the wiry hair on his hands and explore every inch of my found soul match, but freeze instead, my heart in my throat.

Does Jack feel it? His grip tightens on my hands as if he does. Shifters believe in fated mates, but does he?

He releases my hands. The loss is sharp, leaving the world cold in the absence of his touch.

"I'm sorry," he says. "I'm pretty grotesque."

I huff in frustration at his misinterpretation of my actions. *He doesn't know.* And this calling himself ugly and grotesque is offensive.

"You are not grotesque," I say. "There are plenty of beings who don't look human in our world."

"That's kind of you to say that, but it's not like a witch like you would want to associate with things like—"

Annoyance has me speaking faster than my social skills can act. "If you must know, I prefer dating more on the more beastly side."

The room drops into silence, and my cheeks burn in a sudden blush. I didn't mean to blurt that out, however true it is. I *have* dated a full gamut of paranormal beings in the past. And I do prefer it.

"The more beastly side?" For the first time, Jack's voice doesn't sound like he's uncomfortable. Instead, it purrs in amusement.

I shrug, trying to play off the sudden embarrassment. "There's nothing quite like tentacles—"

A disgruntled sound comes from the beast before me, cutting me off. His hands grip mine again, this time lifting before placing them on either side of his face.

I trace my fingers over his cheeks. There's hair here too, it's coarse and thins in places, but the action of petting it feels soothing under my hands. I stop myself from exploring his face but note that he seems to have a shorter snout than that of a wolf.

My curiosity about my fated mate burns, but I do my best to curtail it. I smooth my hands over his cheeks again without realizing it and try to keep from wondering just how wide Jack's shoulders are in this form.

There's the distinct thwacking sound of the wagging of a tail before it stops abruptly.

Behave, Belinda! I'm supposed to be analyzing this pesky curse on my soul mate, not feeling him up.

I take a deep breath and concentrate. The hum of magic reverberates in my mind's eye until it forms threads. Everyone that alters magic with any complexity perceives it in different ways. For me, it's always been threads. I don't know which came first, my love of embroidery or the way magic appears in the form of tangled knots.

Now it's just about untangling the knots.

Jack's own magic from his wolf weaves a silver thread through his presence, his soul a warm glow behind that; magic, but untouchable for one with my skills. The distant threads of my ward on the shop surround us, and I frown.

Where is the curse? I step closer, trying to concentrate. My front brushes the cloth of Jack's jacket and he jumps.

"Sorry, I just need to—there we go!" My front almost presses to his, but I push the sensations away, scanning the threads again.

I'm so close that his minty breath warms my cheek.

I focus hard on the silver thread of Jack's wolf, and it shimmers. *There!* Another thread reveals itself. A dark-green thread winds and knots around the silver thread, so tight it's barely visible to my senses. I frown for a different reason this time. The green thread glints in the way fae spells do, and there is no portion of silver thread that isn't wrapped with it.

I drag my hands down Jack's thick neck, over the sleeker fur there, and dig my fingers into the flesh of his shoulders under his jacket. My magic tugs at the green thread, and Jack gasps. The texture of the curse is slippery, but it gives up its secrets after a few more nudges.

Jack isn't going to like these secrets.

I prod a little more, and Jack's hands that have somehow made their way to my hips tighten. I open my eyes to the world of regular darkness.

Heat bathes my front, and it's clear that I'm violating Jack's personal space, but with the heat comes a twist of arousal in my low belly. My fingers thread decadently through the fur of his neck. The form before me vibrates with the soft rumble of a growl, and I come to my senses. The air between us is thick with tension, and a small part of my mind is satisfied that I'm not the only one feeling this.

But we have things to discuss. I take a step back, and the large hands gripping my hips release me.

"Um, I found it," I say.

"The curse?" Jack asks. I've adjusted to the dark just enough to see two pointed shapes perk up. *Ears.*

I nod. "Uh, yep."

I return to my chair, trying to loosen the interest that tightens my body.

"Do you know why I'm cursed?" The earnestness in his voice breaks my heart, but I keep my face professional.

The first item on the list: deal with the curse. It's Jack's biggest concern and nothing should detract from it. After that's handled, I'll tell Jack that we are soul mates.

"It's fae in origin, but it's hereditary," I say.

"Hereditary?"

"It's as if your line has been cursed. There's no telling how far back it starts or the reasoning behind it." I shrug. "Pre-Council era fae curses can be because of anything from looking at them wrong to doing something actually offensive."

Much of the conflict among the paranormal beings settled with the creation of the Council that rules over us. The system isn't perfect, but the decrease in the number of curses being placed is good for the community, even if it means less work for curse breakers like me.

"Can you break it?" Jack asks.

I wince. "Maybe. I have some methods I want to try before we resort to a riskier one—"

"Yes, anything you have to do, do it." He sounds hopeful.

I try to temper his expectations. "Jack, it might not work."

"I believe in you."

The soulful sound of that declaration has me breathless before dread rises.

"I vow to you that I'll try my hardest."

"Um, how much will your services cost?" he asks.

I freeze. My soul rebels at the idea of accepting money from my mate. "I'm not sure. We can talk about payment plans if you want, or if you have any skills to exchange. I promise you won't be subjecting yourself to eternal servitude," I ramble, and my cheeks heat. "And, hey, if I don't succeed, there's no charge."

His laugh is rich. "We can talk about it later. Eternal servitude wouldn't be too great of a cost to pay."

I snort, but the idea is a sad one. I can't control how clients think of their own afflictions, but later, as his mate, we can talk about whatever insecurities he may have.

Jack is mine to keep, cursed or not.

CHAPTER 5
JACK

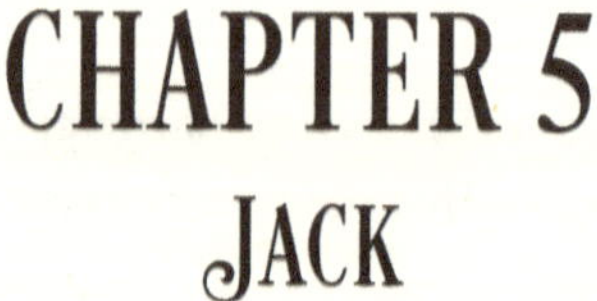

"Watch it!" Broderick calls and ducks at the same time. I curse and try to pay better attention to where I'm maneuvering the lumber in my grip.

"Sorry!" I say, embarrassment burning my cheeks. A construction site is not the place to let my thoughts wander. At least no one can tell I'm blushing under all the fur.

The gargoyle shakes his head, grinning as he grips the end of the wood and helps me slide it where it needs to go. "It's all good. Have something important on your mind? You seem distracted."

I swallow. I don't want to lie to my boss. Well, one of my bosses. The other two have other tasks than the construction work part of the business, though I've seen them both put on hard hats when a deadline gets close.

"I met with another magic practitioner," I say.

Broderick nods. He and his mates gave me a couple of names for curse breakers when I'd started off. The triad of gargoyles run their renovations business unlike any organization I've worked for.

They care deeply for their employees and have been helpful in navigating a world where glamour is needed if you don't look human.

They act like everyone they employ is a part of their family. It's why I feel so awful for being distracted.

"Did you get any good news from them?" Broderick prods.

"It's the same as usual. She has methods she wants to try but is making no promises."

Broderick's mouth curves. "You usually don't walk around in a daze when you meet with a magic practitioner. Anything different about *her*?"

I avoid his gaze. "She's pretty."

Pretty is an understatement. I'd been struck dumb by the sight of Belinda behind the store counter. Her curly dark hair added a level of chaos to her nature. At odds with her delicate features, pouty lips, and warm-amber eyes. The sexy librarian glasses and embroidered fashion tastes proclaimed a sense of her personality before she even greeted me.

"And…" Broderick trails off.

Smart, skilled, generous. All good things to find in a curse breaker. It's the other things about her that distract me. Her enthusiasm is so bright it leaves me blinking, not to mention the searing connection at her touch. It was like nothing I've ever felt before.

This magic practitioner is different. This time feels different.

"She thinks she can help," I say.

"That's good." Broderick hesitates, mulling over what he's going to ask. "So are you going to ask her out?"

I look down at my unglamoured form and push down a shudder of disgust. Ask Belinda out on a date? Like this?

"I don't think she'd say yes," I say instead of shrugging off the question. Of course I want to date her. There's something about her presence that calms my inner beast. When he isn't mentally crying out that we should claim her, that is. I shake my head.

"She might surprise you," Broderick says.

Mate. The inner beast pipes up with another ridiculous statement.

"She might," I respond instead of starting a pity party about why she'd say no. If she broke the curse though…

If I wasn't cursed, I'd ask her out in an instant. Hell, with the way my heart stutters at the thought, I'd find a way to marry her. Something about that resonates in my chest and makes my inner beast happy.

I want Belinda desperately, and the way she'd pressed herself against me makes me wonder if the feeling is mutual. I should court her. I should try.

Because if she does break this curse…

I continue working. My heart is a little lighter at the concept that things aren't quite so impossible.

I have hope.

CHAPTER 6
BELINDA

Focus is my superpower and I throw everything I have into trying to break Jack's curse. I assemble books about wolf shifter transformations and fae spells. I even throw a book on lycanthropes in the pile, though, according to the text, that subspecies of fae haven't been sighted in the last hundred years. I'm skeptical about that tidbit because rarer species are notoriously secretive, but all information is helpful information.

Every interaction we have, I'm tempted to blurt out that we're soul mates, but that confession will derail everything, and Jack wants this curse broken so badly.

Maybe I won't even have to tell him.

Maybe he'll recognize that we're fated mates.

Every few days, I muster up the research and materials to try for a solution less extreme than my last resort, and I call my soul mate. Our conversations are awkward at first. We're strangers meeting under less-than-ideal circumstances, but slowly that changes.

"I'm starting to think that these calls are just because you miss me," he teases over the phone a week into our process.

"Oh, I definitely miss you, but I do have another idea." My words sound much less like teasing than his did.

There's a pause over the phone, and I want to fill it, but don't trust myself to stay on the topic of curses.

My soul cries out for Jack. Does he feel the same? Is this one sided?

I don't think it is.

That attempt and a few others fail, but I keep at it.

When Jack shows up at the shop, my heart swoops at the sight of him and the antsy nerves at his absence subside.

"I'm glad you could stop by," I say, leading us to the sitting area in the back of the shop. The shelves are tall enough to block us from any passerby. I don't want to go into my workroom if it can be helped. I still haven't properly seen Jack's true form and I can tell he doesn't want me to.

The first attempts to break the curse were things that other magical practitioners have tried before but that I wanted to eliminate just in case. I've chanted over the man, had him meditate, and waved burning herbs over his body, sensing the strums of the magic threads each time, but the curse holds tight.

I've attempted other ways of breaking the curse since then. Methods listed in old books I've consulted. My hopes are high for this potion. The recipe came from a very detailed account of a wolf shifter refusing to return to their human form. Something about the herb mixture is supposed to make the *wolf* part of shifters sleep.

We sit, and I hand Jack the stoppered bottle of herb mixture. It's mainly the color of trampled leaves with an off-putting green smell.

"Okay, try drinking this," I say. Preparing myself to cite what's in it and why I think this could work, but as with all the things we've tried so far, Jack downs the mixture without hesitation.

His human face scrunches in disgust, and I feel my own sympathetic stomach retch a little.

After a moment, his face eases, but his lips are still tight. "I don't want to insult you, but that is foul."

I laugh in relief. "Next time, I'll put sugar in it."

He perks up. "Really?"

"No," I say.

He laughs, and a sound has me leaning forward. Jack's eyes glint wolfishly as if taking in our distance before his face softens.

"Thank you, Bel."

I blink, still not used to the intimate way he shortens my name. "I haven't done anything yet. We'll give the remedy a minute to work, and I'll check the magic then."

His mouth twists in disappointment. "I imagine I'd be able to feel if it's working."

I shrug with a wince. "Most likely."

Jack shakes the bitterness away from his shoulders. "Thank you for trying so hard."

I frown. I'd try this hard with anyone who would come to me for help, but I have a vested interest in making Jack happy.

He continues. "These last couple weeks, I've been poked and prodded, tasted more horrible potions than I ever want to in my life, and had you whispering incantations in my ear for so long I think I'm starting to dream about them."

"I care, Jack." I bite my tongue to keep from spilling everything. "And all of those things didn't work."

"Yes, but you're trying, and for the first time in a long time, I'm hopeful. It feels like I have a future again. Almost like I can make plans," Jack says. He places his hand on mine, which rests on my knee, his fingers intertwining with mine. The touch soothes the worries that plague me of what will happen if I fail to break his curse. "Like I could maybe ask a certain witch out on a date if this all goes well."

My heart flutters in my chest. "If I'm not that certain witch, I may turn you into something fouler than that potion."

Jack's laugh is hearty now, and I can't stop the burn of my blush any more than I could keep that statement to myself.

"Consider me warned, but I don't think that's something we'll have to worry about." The warm, hungry look in his eyes takes my breath away.

The attempt is a failure and though Jack tries to hide his disappointment, it hangs in the air.

"There are so many options left," I say.

Jack smiles sadly. "I trust you."

He goes to leave but stops as if he's arguing with himself before turning back.

"I know that I'm currently something out of nightmares, but can I take you out for coffee?" The question is rough, as if he's rusty at dating.

My happiness glosses over his self-denigration.

"I'd love that!"

CHAPTER 7
JACK

"So what do you do for fun?" Belinda asks, gesturing with her french fry.

I smile at the sight she makes, my primal side taking hearty satisfaction in gifting her food. It's like a loophole in my mind. This isn't a lunch date, but it's close enough to appease my inner beast.

And I get to spend more time with her.

I brought us lunch when she said that she had something for me to pick up. The thrilled look on her face when I'd presented her with the greasy burgers and fries is one that will stay with me till the end of time.

"Are you sure you don't want me to just go?" I ask, trying to be careful of overstaying my welcome. She'd only asked me to come by to give me a crystal to keep on my person for the next several days.

Belinda rolls her eyes. "No! I like to spend time with you."

My heart swells at that. She'd gone to the café down the street with me last time, and it'd been awkward at first. I hadn't taken anyone out in such a long time, but Belinda thawed me with her excitement and the easy way she'd touch my human glamour.

Each stroke of her fingers on my hand and the casual way she slid in the seat next to me had my inner beast whispering all sorts of inappropriate things in my head. *Ours. Take her. Breed her. Claim her. Home.*

Each whisper isn't as distracting as the creature usually is. In Bel's presence, it's both easier and harder to ignore it. Easier because her minty sage scent and bright laugh catch all of my attention and harder because the whispers make me want.

I can hardly wait for her to break this curse. It seems impossible to me that she'll fail with how devoted she is to the task.

"What do I do for fun?" I repeat her question, and my cheeks burn. "I'm a cliché, but I'm a man who likes video games."

Bel's eyes glint with teasing. "What kind of video games? Do you spend days competing against twelve-year-olds?"

My laugh is easy. "Not days, and I have a group of adults I play with. Those twelve-year-olds are fierce competition. I like the party games so that I can talk to other people without having to wear a glamour."

Belinda's grin is warm and free from pity, as if I didn't just confess a limitation. "You'll have to teach me to play sometime."

My throat swells. "I'd love to."

CHAPTER 8
ᏟBELINDA

Coffee dates and gifted lunches every time I attempt to break his curse are how I get to know my soul mate. I'm trying my best not to get distracted from my task, but he's so *distracting*. Every moment together inspires temptation. I try to stick to facts instead of letting myself give in to temptation and lean into his space or touch him.

One of those facts is that he works in construction with other beings that require glamour in their everyday life. There's a tiny surge of jealousy that the people Jack works with see him in his most honest form, and I haven't, but I stuff down the inappropriate feeling.

"But you have a glamour," I say, gesturing to his human form. "You could work anywhere you want, right?"

Jack grimaces. "This type of glamour isn't cheap. If I wear it less often, I can stretch it further."

"Oh," I say, thinking of all the time we've spent chatting together. It never occurred to me that it was costing Jack to appear human around me.

"And I actually enjoy working there. My coworkers feel like… family." Jack's cheeks pinken.

"They've become your pack," I say.

"Exactly." The skin around his eyes crinkles. "It's funny. In a lot of ways, my life is more promising now than before the curse."

The look in his gold eyes is direct and heavy. "How so?"

"Well, I found one thing I didn't know I was looking for."

I bite my lip at his words. Jack changes the subject before I get too excited.

Too distracted.

There are moments where our hands touch or gazes meet that leave me blushing. I make a clumsy advance, or two, or three, asking him to come up to my apartment over the shop, but he resists. I may be waiting to address the fact that we're mates until after the curse is broken, but that doesn't mean I don't want him.

"I can't, Bel," he says.

"Why?"

"I don't want what we have to be tainted by my curse. You deserve the best of me, not to be pawed at because my wolf wants to devour you. It's already a struggle to remain civilized around you."

My body sways toward him. "I wouldn't mind being—"

"Not yet, Belinda. Please."

I nod. We have the rest of our lives together. I just need to break Jack's curse. But the days pass, and I don't know how realistic breaking the curse is anymore. The cloud of disappointment and sadness over Jack seems to grow with every failure.

"You've been trying your hardest for weeks, Bel. I don't want to waste your time if this is a fool's errand," he says.

"Waste my time? You are not a waste of time. You're my—" I shake my head. "You're mine."

The words are accurate without revealing more than Jack's ready to accept. The expression on his human-appearing face is full of vulnerability.

"You've tried so many methods. Why can't we just try the one you mentioned when we first met?" he asks.

"It's risky—"

"But it's the most promising, isn't it?"

I don't want to lie to him. "Yes."

"I think it's time to try. I don't want to disrupt your life if—" He cuts himself off with a look of helplessness. *Disrupt my life?*

"Jack, if I can't lift the curse, I'll still want to be—"

"How is it risky?" His question is rushed, as if he's not ready to hear such a declaration.

He's not ready to know we're soul mates.

I straighten my spine. "The method would be me manipulating the magic. I'd carefully untangle the curse strand by strand and hopefully pull it free from you."

Hope flares in his face at that.

"But if I can't get a grip on the thread, if I lose it... the curse could become permanent." I shrug hollowly.

"Belinda, I—" Jack breaks himself off and swallows. The price of this option is too high. It's why I didn't want to resort to it without exhausting all other methods.

"But if that's what happens, if I don't break your curse, I want you to know—" I start.

I'm cut off by his kiss. The crash of his lips against mine levels and revitalizes me. I moan into his mouth eagerly when his tongue slips into mine and firecrackers of sensation rain down my spine.

I'm panting when we part.

"It's worth the risk," Jack says, his eyes full of weight and purpose, as if to say *you're worth the risk.*

I pull in oxygen, but when I respond, my voice is still breathless. "It's your choice to make."

Which is how I find myself stumbling in the dark of my workroom, trying to make a warding circle. My eyes have mostly adjusted to the low light, but I avert them out of respect for Jack's privacy even as curiosity eats away my conviction.

I wish he'd trust that his form isn't going to disgust me.

But trust comes with time.

I stand straight. The ward I've made in the dark surrounds the chair that holds Jack's large form. I take a few deep breaths and run my fingers over the witchy skulls I'd embroidered on the cuffs of my sleeves to center myself.

It takes a minute of brushing against the threaded detail before the tension in my shoulders seeps finally from me and my heart calms.

"Are you ready?" I ask.

"Please," Jack says. "And then we can go out on a real date."

His upbeat words don't hide the naked hunger in his voice. The flavor of it has my heart cracking, and I screw my eyes shut. Warmth envelops my cheek and rough, padded calluses press, cradling my face as if to reassure me. I cup my palm around Jack's hand, bathing in this rare contact.

"Hey, Bel, please don't stress. I know that this may not work. If it doesn't—" I hear him swallow. "If I'm stuck like this, I know you did everything you possibly could."

The sharp ends of his claws prick my skin as he pulls away.

I sniff and nod. "Well, either way, you owe me dinner after this."

"Bel—"

I make a cutting gesture with my hand, and he stops. "You owe me this real date you've been teasing me about."

His chuckle is full of disbelief.

I shake my head and raise my hands in front of me. "Let's get this show on the road."

Jack's hands take mine and bring my palms to his face. Nerves threaten to push up my heart rate and I let my fingers run over the shapes of his features to center myself for this task.

"Okay," I say and close my eyes. "Don't interrupt me."

"Yes, my mate," he chuffs before stiffening.

I shut down the flip of my stomach at those words and push forward. Now is not the time to be distracted by his telling slip. *He knows,* my mind crows. *That doesn't matter right now,* I reason back. Right now, I need to focus on breaking my mate's curse.

The world in my mind comes alight with magic and tangles of threads. I'm quicker to find the threads of the curse now that I know what I'm looking for. Sure enough, the silvery woven thread of Jack's wolf is bright and pulses under my touch as if his beast wants to loop around me to keep me close.

My mouth curves at that and I focus harder to see the dark-green thread choking around the silver. The curse.

Slowly, as if I have tweezers, I use my own magic to tug on the green thread. As before, the fae magic is resistant but eventually yields. I keep my breathing measured, cautious as I start to pull the magic from the silver of Jack.

The wolf shifter under my hands shivers at the sensation, but I block it out and focus on the first knot of the curse. The knot is around several silver threads, and I wind the magic I've already collected around my finger so it doesn't slip away before snipping it.

"The crystal, please." My voice is hoarse. My energy is already starting to wane. There's movement, and the layered texture of the rock slides against my palm. I fist my hand around the crystal, feeding the threads into the storage device before easing my grip. "Take it back."

Jack does as I say, and I focus on the knot in front of me, untangling it slowly until the silver threads spring apart, and I pinch the end of the green thread with all my might, continuing to spool the magic as I follow the thread until I meet another knot. I repeat the process a few times.

Sweat runs down my spine and I gasp in exertion. Every so often, Jack makes a pained sound that he cuts off.

The pull of the magic I'm working with is costing me an uncommon amount of energy, as if what I'm doing is against the grain, wrong.

Everything blurs before me.

"No, no, no," I whisper, waiting for the vision of the threads to come back into focus. It looks like there's one more knot. One more knot, and I can give Jack exactly what he wants. The thread bites deeper into my magic, resisting.

Exhaustion pulls me down. I've truly overextended myself, but if I stop now, I'll never find these specific threads again. With the way I've been yanking at it, it could very well snap and be absorbed into Jack's threads, becoming a part of his very essence.

I sway on my feet, and Jack's hands grip me, keeping me upright. My vision of the threads come into focus, and I quickly untangle the last knot.

I'm about to take a relieved breath when the thread I grip is yanked away out of my hand, and I lose track of it.

"No!" I scramble for it, but it's gone. The world of threads blurs and blinks out.

I've failed. I fall and the world goes dark.

I wake in the arms of my mate. The room is still dark, but I know the sensation of his presence and the scent of fresh-cut cedar.

"Jack—" I croak.

"Shh, drink."

A glass is pressed to my lips, and the cold water soothes my throat.

"Are you okay?" he asks.

I try and think back to how I got here. Trying to break the curse... and failing.

No, I'm not okay. The aches in my body and soul tell me that I used up every bit of energy trying to lift the curse, and it wasn't enough.

"H-how long was I out?" I rasp.

"A few minutes. You were working on it for hours."

Tears well in my eyes, and I try to keep from sobbing.

Jack makes a sound similar to a canine whine. "Bel, beautiful Bel. Please don't cry."

I shake my head and press my face into the fur at Jack's neck.

"Don't think about it," Jack says.

But I can't stop thinking about it.

My sobs are quiet, but Jack holds me tightly. He comforts me while the truth of what happened ricochets through me.

I've failed my mate. Jack will have to live with how I've disappointed him for the rest of his life.

The pain of that is like a vise around my heart. I push myself out of his arms, trying to breathe through it. We need to talk. I've disappointed him, but I need to figure out how to persist past that. But first—

"It didn't work," I say.

The shadowy form of my mate shrugs as if it doesn't matter. "You tried."

"I was able to get a lot of it. You might not need to worry about passing the curse on to your children," I mumble.

Jack hesitates. "Belinda, the kind of life with children, isn't in the cards for me."

"What kind of life?" I ask. Prickles of unease run over my skin.

The silence grows between us, and icy panic stirs.

"I know this isn't the answer you were hoping for." I sniff, scrubbing the tears from my face.

The shadows move and I get the sense that he's shaking his head. I can practically taste his sadness in the air. I place my hand over the furry knuckles and claws on the armrest, and he pulls away. I'm carefully placed on the chair. Already I miss being held by him.

"We tried, Bel," he says. "You tried so hard, but... it's not in the cards for us."

"No," I say. The word is choked but so harsh it hurts my throat.

But Jack is pulling away from me. "Bel—I'm so fucking sorry."

"Don't go!" I try to grab hold of our future together, but it's like trying to catch smoke. "I-I thought we were going to go to dinner?"

Stupid, stupid, stupid. He's not going to want to go out. Not when he's dealing with the permanency of his curse.

"Bel… that's not possible."

I want to throw myself at him, dig my fingers into his fur and make him stay, but I can hardly stand.

"Your glamour—" I try instead.

"Is just a glamour!" Jack shouts. Frustration and grief are clear in his voice and his next words are softer. "I'm still a monster under it."

"But I want your monster," I whisper.

Jack steps toward me with a growl. The primal energy coming off him makes me want to run and throw myself at him in equal measure.

"My wolf wants to ravish you, lock you away from the world." His voice is low, and my attention is rapt. "I'm barely in control as it is."

"Then let him! We're mates!" I blurt out what we both know by now.

"We can't be mates when I'm *this*."

The large, clawed hand gestures to his body.

"*Please!*" I say. "We can figure something out. I like you the way you are."

"I can't." His words hit with the finality of a guillotine and the panic buzzing in my mind silences into despair.

The door clicks when he leaves. My fated mate is gone.

He left me.

My heart bleeds pain as if I've been grievously wounded.

I sit in the dark and cry.

CHAPTER 9
BELINDA
PRESENT

Fear and something I can't quite name flow through my blood as I run. I am afraid but this isn't a cougar or a bear. My panicking body recognizes what I'm running from, even if my mind hasn't yet. The pounding of my feet on the ground and the rush of air against my skin are a primal dance I've never participated in.

Another howl sounds behind me, closer.

I ignore how the underbrush tears at my tights and the pebbles bruise my feet, my sandals long gone. Something large crashes behind me.

I scream when I trip, but instead of slamming into the ground, I'm caught.

Clawed hands seize me, and familiarity rises past my panic. There's no time to make sense of anything because we're still moving at a run. The world blurs as I'm flung upward, over a broad shoulder that jostles me with every loping stride. My fingers dig into a fur-covered back before my brain catches up to the fact that I've been snatched. I beat my fists against the back under me.

"Let me go!" My shout is only met by a growl. The light scent of cut cedar has misplaced heat kindling instead of fear.

"Jack?" I ask. It defies logic, but my heart knows I'm right.

We slow when the trees break into a small clearing. I'm tossed to the ground and stumble back, falling on my ass. I barely catch sight of Jack's "monstrous" form before he flips me onto all fours, one of those giant clawed hands pressing between my shoulder blades, grinding my chest into the dirt.

I struggle, but it's no use. I'm pinned.

"Jack!" I shout. Annoyance and frustration rush to the surface. And anger.

"Mate." The word is a growl so deep it's hard to make it out. Is this his wolf speaking? The primal part of his animal that can't be separated from a shifter.

"Yes! I know! But you can't just chase me down like a fucking deer!"

Another growl. "You're in another male's territory. His pheromones are everywhere."

"I know!" I growl back. "He's my date!"

The silence that falls over us has teeth that tear and rip into me no matter the fact that I've done nothing wrong. Jack's snarl breaks the stillness and has the hair on the back of my neck standing up.

"No! You're my mate," he says.

I grit my teeth at him using the m-word again. My anger morphs into fury.

"Why should you care?" I spit. "You're the one that left me!"

There's a pause, and the long-fingered hand on my back tenses and relaxes, as if Jack's struggling.

"It was the right thing to do." The words are less growly this time.

"No!" I try to lift my chest from the dirt. "I called you over and over again, trying to convince you to be with me. Well, guess what, I'm not trying anymore. I need to move on, and this date is the first of many."

"I can't. I can't let you go." The growl is back as if the civilized part of him has lost this round. Jack presses his hips against my raised ass. "Mine."

I moan. The adrenaline from the run and being pinned and helpless has me heating for all the wrong reasons.

"Wrong," I whisper. "I *was* yours, and you threw me away."

The pain of him leaving me in my workroom, helpless to follow because I could barely stand, still ricochets through me.

A thick tongue licks the back of my neck and ear. An unholy heat cascades over me, and Jack rocks his large form against my hips again. There are only a few layers of fabric separating my wet pussy from the hard bulge pressing against it.

The devious part of me wants to push back against Jack's body, to tempt the beast behind me into giving me what we've been skirting around since the first moment we met.

A hungry growl rumbles over my nerves as if Jack can read my mind.

"Mine. I can taste your desire," he says, his words almost slurring. "I need to satisfy my mate."

My anger still crackles under my skin, along with my arousal. "Oh, that's rich. Now you want to satisfy me? You had your chance, Jack."

My skirt is pushed up despite my words, and the sound of ripping fills the air. I cry out, and I can't tell if it's from annoyance or desperation. My tights and panties pull against my skin as they rip until the cold forest air hits my ass and the wetness between my legs.

Fuck. I liked that too much.

Jack grips the back of my neck to keep me in place as his body moves behind me until his hot breath hits my pussy. We moan in unison when he licks me. His tongue is strong, long, and pointed in a very noncanine way. The next stroke has me pushing my hips back at him.

It suddenly doesn't matter that Jack broke my heart, that he rejected me, that I failed to break his curse. All that matters now is the stroke of that hot tongue and the possessive grip on the back of my neck. Each erotic action clicks into place how we should have been as if they sweep away every wrong he's ever done to me.

As if I've already forgiven him.

My mate.

"Don't stop," I gasp, my body capitulating to him.

Jack's moan is rough and the sounds that fall from my lips would make me blush if I were in my right mind. The slide of his tongue is a deliverance from the terrible time since we'd last parted. The constant tears, the catatonic grief. I'd finally emotionally dealt with my personal shame of not being able to break Jack's curse. It had taken time to come to terms with the fact that I'd done the best I could.

The pain of Jack's rejection… I'd thought a hard fuck may get me on the right path. This isn't the hard fuck I'd had in mind, but I'm starving for his touch.

"Please, Jack," I say. I don't know exactly what I'm begging for yet, but I know I need it.

Jack grips the back of my neck harder when I twist against his mouth.

"Please, please, please." My begs are whispers of my soul's most fervent wish.

"You're on a date." He groans the words and there is still a thread of anger there.

"But I want you. I always want you," I say.

The pleased sound he makes tells me how much he likes that. He slides his tongue inside me as a reward, and I shout.

"So good—" I break off on a cry as his tongue curls inside me. My need is heavy, and I shamelessly shove my pussy back into his mouth with as much abandon as I can manage while being pinned.

Each stroke hits me exactly where I need it, but it's not enough.

"Jack, I need you."

His tongue slides from me, and I make a sound of loss.

"Bel, you're so perfect," he says. "Mine."

Mine. Yes, that's what I want.

"Claim me," I say.

Jack's growl is deeper at my request, and he pulls away from me, motions jarring and primal. I whimper at the loss, but it's cut off at the slick-on-slick sound behind me. I turn my head, but Jack blocks the motion, stopping me from assuaging my curiosity. I cease trying to see him at the wet smack of a thick weight on my back.

I moan as what feels like a giant blunt tongue slides over my ass. A tongue, but too thick, too hard. The member drags lower, smearing the wetness it's covered in over my skin. The blunt head of him pokes against me as if Jack can't help the rocking of his hips even if he's not where he needs to be yet.

"Oh gods," I say when the head of his cock presses against my pussy. I'm so soft and wet there that the flesh yields to him, sliding him to my entrance.

Jack freezes as the movement of his hips presses the shape of him barely inside me. The back of my neck is released, and his hands grip my hips instead as if to stop me from moving or to stop himself from thrusting forward.

"Belinda, don't move." Jack's voice sounds tortured as if he's only now realizing where this was leading.

"No! I need you," I beg.

He growls. "You don't need to fuck a beast."

I smack the ground in frustration. "Yes, I do! I need you inside me. I need you to fuck me."

"I'm a monst—"

"If you don't fuck me, I'll find someone who will!" I threaten as if I can just walk away from this without leaving my heart bleeding on the ground.

The snarl rent from him is loud and completely inhuman. I'm about to snarl back when my mate thrusts forward.

I shout but can barely hear it over the rush of blood in my ears. Everything clears from my mind except the animalistic sensation of being taken by my mate.

Oh, holy gods! The stretch!

Jack's howl is triumphant.

His body moves again into mine. I groan as the heavy cock forges its way deeper inside me.

"Oh, fuuuuck…" I trail off when he slides out before thrusting in again.

This time my ass hits the base of him. The hair on his body and thighs tickles my skin. He freezes with his body fully encased in the wrap of mine.

"Oh Jack," I gasp. The cock inside of me throbs as I stretch around it, willing my body to accept every inch of him.

"God, Bel. You're taking it all, aren't you?" Jack asks.

Over my gasping breaths, my body screams in its need for release. I writhe for relief and find none.

"I need you to move, Jack."

His claws dig into my hips.

"I need you to fuck me," I beg.

Those are the right words to say because my monster ruts into me then.

"Mine," he snarls. "Mine to fill, mine to breed. My mate."

My body heats and slicks to meet my mate. To take from him what he'll give me.

It doesn't matter that I'm wearing a charm to ward against pregnancy. He can try to breed me into the ground if he wants.

The rutting motion is fast and jarring, but my body rises to meet it. Pleasure heightens with each drag and thrust inside me. The waves of my arousal push me higher and higher.

Jack gives me his full cock again, up to the base of him, and holds me there with a groan. The first splash of liquid heat triggers my climax, and I struggle, trying to thrust my body back against Jack, but he keeps me motionless. The thickening of his cock only throws me further into ecstasy.

"Oh! What—" I start.

"My knot," he gasps.

"Your what?!" I twist to look at my mate, but the motion tugs at the swollen *knot* inside me, and we both hiss.

I moan as the knot gets even bigger. It triggers something in me. *Claim, claim, claim,* my instincts whisper. I tilt my head to the side, my forehead grinding into the dirt as I attempt to bare my neck completely.

Our bodies throb in time to each other. My heartbeat starts to slow, and I wait for the action that will officially make us mates by shifter standards.

I wait for my mating bite.

The silence of the forest ebbs away and I can hear crickets in the distance, and still, I wait.

The trance of instinct wrapped around my mind cracks.

"Jack?" I ask.

He huffs.

"Claim me," I say.

And still, he doesn't move. A minute passes, and then another. The heat of our connected bodies cools. The knot connecting us softens, and he slides from me.

I want to curl in on myself and cradle the empty place in me, but I don't move. If Jack is going to reject me again, I'm going to make him say it.

"Jack," I say.

"No."

I squeeze my eyes shut to keep my tears from falling.

"I can't," he says.

It doesn't matter that the words are soft. They wound me. I yielded to him. I gave up my body for him and it still isn't enough.

"Can't or won't?" My voice is hoarse, and I don't wait for the answer. I press up to kneeling and pull my dress down, ignoring the river of seed running down my thigh.

The warmth of Jack's furred body moves away from me, and I wipe a tear away with a sniff.

"Bel, it's not that I don't want you."

"I think that's exactly what it is."

"Look at me!" The volume and pain of his voice startles me. "I'm a monster!"

I finally let myself look at him. A being similar to the werewolves found in Hollywood movies stands on hind legs with arms spread, waiting for my inspection. He's big, tall with strong shoulders and long limbs. His body is covered with fur that thins in places and thickens into a tail behind him. His face isn't much of a surprise. The truncated snout with large fangs and yellow eyes.

I recognize him. Even stuck in the form he's in, there's a familiarity to the slope of his brow, the shape of his eyes. Or maybe it's just that my heart sings in his presence. My soul recognizes my other half.

Jack casts his gaze away from me. "And I'd be even worse if I trapped you as my mate for the rest of your life."

I want to grab him by the shoulders and shake him. "I've already told you that I like that about you! I like your wolf being so close to the surface! Your wolf has never hurt me!"

"I just chased you down and fucked you in the dirt!" Anger seeps into Jack's voice.

"I wanted that. I trust your wolf. He knows what he wants," I say.

Jack scoffs, and I continue. "He wouldn't abandon his mate once he found her. It's the man I don't trust!"

Jack's ears flatten as if in pain, and I cut my gaze away. I need to focus on other things. I need to keep moving.

"Where the fuck is my phone?" *Fuck.* There's some sort of paranormal being going into heat and I'm not going to be able to show up with my thighs streaked with the seed of my almost-not-quite ex. "I need to call someone about my date."

A growl rumbles from the fierce beast in front of me and my anger snaps.

"Oh, fuck you! You don't even want me."

"I want you too much, but I can't—"

My sneer cuts him off. I abandon my search for my phone and march up to him, poking his chest. "You. Don't. Want. Me. Enough. You won't listen to me and what I want. You're cursed. You're never going to look or be like how you were before, and I am so sorry, but I want to be with you just the way you are—"

"You should find someone better," he says adamantly.

I hold in my hiss of anger. "You are my mate. My soul mate. I know this. There isn't anyone I want more."

"Not even the guy whose pheromones are hanging in the woods?"

"That was—" I blink away the rush of emotion and continue with a whisper. "That was a mistake."

There is no way to fuck away the ache for this beast. Not even the promise of heat sex with an interestingly shaped cock can remedy the wound of this rejection. I know myself well enough to admit defeat.

Jack stands motionless, his hands twitching as if he wants to grab hold of me.

I shake my head, walking a couple steps away before gazing up to the starry sky as if for guidance. I'm angry and hurt, but it's all underlined with devastation.

I turn toward a frozen Jack and spread my arms. "What do I have to do to prove that I want you the way you are?"

My voice cracks and that's what spurs me on, makes me want to lash out. I need Jack. It's only fair that he should feel the same way about me.

"Is it that you want me to beg?" I ask. "Am I going to need to spread my legs in front of you, show you how wet I am?"

The tension in the air thickens with my words, and Jack's eyes glint in the moonlight. The look in his eyes makes me want to do wicked things. Mean things. Things that taunt my soul mate into forgetting the weight of his negative self-talk.

I pull the zipper of the dress down and let the garment fall first from my shoulders and then from my hips before stepping out of it. The beast before me freezes. I'm completely bared to him. I'd forgone a bra, and he'd already torn free my panties. I kick my dress flat before lowering myself to it and lying back.

The positioning under the moon makes me look like a sacrifice.

I prop myself up as a thought occurs to me. "Why are you even here, Jack? Did you follow me?"

He shakes his head. "I came here for a run and caught your scent on the wind. I needed to make sure you were safe, but when I saw you—when I scented the male—"

Chance. Fate.

I gaze up at the moon. My wolf requires more convincing that we're meant to be. I slide my hands up over my breasts, and Jack's glowing yellow eyes follow the movement.

"Belinda..." Jack trails off. He swallows as I display everything he's letting go of.

"I want you, Jack. There's nothing about your form that disgusts me."

"You can't want this," he says.

I hum. "I'm getting pretty annoyed that you don't believe me. Does the fact that I want you this way disgust you? Is that what the issue is?"

"Of course not! I want to be the best version of myself for you."

I swallow at that. "And you don't think I want to be the best version of myself for you? We both have our perceived flaws, but at this moment, I'm telling you that I want you how you are."

I slide a hand down and spread my legs, placing my feet flat on the ground and bending my knees. I stroke up my folds, and the sound of my wetness has a hungry growl rumbling from Jack.

The motion is almost meditative with a spike of pleasure, and I let myself fall into it.

"Under this moon, I offer you my body, my soul, for claiming. Will you reject me?" I swallow. The moment is heavy with the weight of tradition and significance. If he denies my offering, there will be no future for us. We'll leave this forest and go our separate ways.

Jack's body tenses as if the truth in my head also echoes in his.

I circle my clit, and my breath shortens. Jack takes a step forward and stops.

"I want you, Jack. I want to see you when you take me." *When you claim me.* The thought is too tender to voice.

That same wet-on-wet sound comes as the head of a fleshy cock unsheathes from the fur of his hips.

I watch it breathlessly, the circling of my finger on myself making my toes curl as inch by inch extends from him.

"This is what you wanted?" he asks, his voice rough with frustration.

I moan as precum beads on the pink head of his cock. Jack tilts his head, considering me.

"You do want this." His words are soft, almost marveling. His long fingers curl around the thick flesh of his cock, careful of his claws. When he strokes up, my legs draw in and a needy sound falls from my lips.

Jack narrows his eyes at me. "You want everything I have to offer you. You're spreading your legs for me, teasing me with how good you smell. It's heady, smelling the mix of my spend leaking from you."

I tremble, and Jack continues. "You want me to fuck you into the dirt again."

"Yes," I whisper.

My cheeks burn and I pinch my nipple. I'm impossibly wet between my legs, a combination of us. I press two fingers in and inhale at the easy slide. My hips tilt up for his gaze.

"I want you to claim me," I say.

Jack breaks the scene for a moment to shake his head slowly in awed disbelief before resuming whatever sacrificial tradition we've started.

"Will you accept my body into yours?" he asks.

I exhale and swallow. My lower body feels heavy with want and I pull my legs wider.

The cock in Jack's hand lengthens and my body clenches on emptiness. He approaches me, falling to his knees before my splayed thighs, tugging his considerable thickness even longer.

How did that fit inside me before? I don't let myself ruminate on that thought. I need to take my mate. I need to prove myself. I need to be claimed.

"Please," I beg.

Jack runs the head of his already shiny cock up my folds. The hot, wet touch has me whimpering.

"*My mate*," he says as if in prayer before he continues in filth. "All open and offering yourself up to me. You're so pretty like this, all pink and wet in the moonlight."

"Jack, I need you," I gasp.

"You need me to fuck you?"

"I need you to stay with me," I say. My emotions are so close to the surface like this. I'm all aroused vulnerability and heartfelt earnestness. "I need you to wake up next to me in the morning and to get takeout together at night. My heart needs you."

Jack bows his head. "I need you too."

"Then make me your mate."

Jack rolls his hips forward and the head of his cock presses in. The stretch of my body is slow this time. He freezes at my hiss of pain.

"No, keep going. You're just so big. I can take you." I run my words together, afraid that he'll pull away from me, but he doesn't.

Jack strokes my cheek. "Shh, I'm not going anywhere. I know you can take your mate."

I moan at that and his cock slides deeper before stopping to pull back some and returning to go farther. Jack works his body into mine. His flesh, my flesh, our souls made to never be separated.

The small thrusts bring him more into my body. Our foreheads meet on one last deep slide that brings my body flush with his. The stretch of cradling him encompasses all my senses. The moment is perfection. All the pain and grief from before are eased by the raw feeling of completeness.

I moan and tense around the impossible amount of Jack inside me.

His voice rumbles from him. "I could die happy from the sweet squeeze of your cunt."

"Jack..." I beg, squirming from the unforgiving fullness.

He moans and our eyes meet. "Mine."

"Yours." I lift my chin. "If you claim me."

Jack narrows his eyes and slowly pulls from me. The drag of his thickness against my inner walls has me moaning, I break off on a cry when he snaps his hips forward, plowing into my body without mercy. He repeats the drag and conquering thrust, moving in an unmerciful rhythm. I lose more and more of my sanity with each move, my fingers clawing into his shoulders as he fucks me.

Jack starts grinding the pad of his thumb against my clit and I try to writhe away from the friction, but he doesn't let me escape. Instead, he pushes me higher until my release breaks over me. I cry out, my body clasping down on his unforgiving girth as pleasure surges in my blood.

"Bel, my Belinda," Jack snarls in satisfaction before truly beginning to fuck me.

He ruts into me, and I take his body eagerly. Each cleaving thrust prolongs my release until Jack thrusts all the way in and halts on a growl.

My moan is guttural as what must be his knot swells against my insides, locking us together. The heat of his cum spills inside me, increasing the tantalizing pressure. The assurance that I've been filled to the brim with his seed.

"My mate," he growls and grips my hair, pulling my head to the side to bare my neck.

The bite is quick, the pain is a flash before the magic of our bond soothes it and throws me into a euphoric release. The world shatters and my grip of reality slips, but I'm exactly where I need to be.

In my mate's arms.

CHAPTER 10
BELINDA

I return to my senses, lying belly down on something warm that rises in a steady rhythm. I blink and Jack's chest comes into focus. The grayish tint to his skin and sparse fur is a comfort. He hasn't hidden under a glamour.

Jack strokes my back, and I enjoy his heart beating against mine. My body is empty, so the knot must have released us while I was passed out from the bond snapping into place.

The soreness in my neck from the mating bond has awe-filled happiness swelling in me. I slide a hand to the wound and sure enough, the bite mark is raised, rapidly healing to be a scar for me to display.

"I'm glad you've accepted that I love you this way," I say.

The chest under me huffs in a laugh. "How could I possibly doubt you after what happened? You argued your point very convincingly."

I tuck my face into his chest to hide my blush. I'm as sexually liberated as the next witch, but I don't think I've ever been as bold as I was when taunting my mate.

Jack pinches my chin and lifts my gaze to his. I'm not completely used to seeing his true face, but each time I do, my comfort grows. The snout, fangs, and pointed ears are Jack. My Jack.

"I'm so sorry I hurt you," he says, the misery clear in his voice. "I'm sorry that I was so stuck in my own head and stubborn about what I thought you should have that I didn't listen to what you wanted. What I did is inexcusable."

I prop myself up on my elbows, my naked breasts rubbing against his skin, but Jack doesn't leer. His gaze is solemn on mine.

"We all have our hang-ups. Thank you for apologizing." I stroke a finger up the bridge of his nose up to his tufted ears. My mind categorizes the shape of them as strange before I go on teasingly. "I may need some more groveling before I accept your apology though."

"Is that so?" Jack says with a mock growl, his hands squeezing my ass, pressing my spread legs against his middle. "I hope to use my tongue to be very convincing."

I moan at the contact and my cheeks burn at the thought of that strong tongue.

Wait. The workings of my brain are slow with how my body hums with tired satisfaction. *If Jack's shift was halted, wouldn't his features be either canine or human?* My eyes sharpen on him with a more clinical gaze, and I sit up, straddling my mate.

I've never analyzed Jack's true appearance in our previous meetings because of his reluctance, his shame. I let myself take in the details now, adding each one to a list of observations. Instead of being flat like a canine, his tongue is long and pointed. The small things add up: the shape of his ears are thicker points, the broadness of his shoulders exceeds that of his human appearance, and do wolf shifters have knots?

After my inspection, which makes Jack raise an eyebrow in question, I have my conclusions.

Well, fuck me. I snort.

"I know why I couldn't break the curse," I say.

Jack frowns down at me. "You don't need to worry—"

I cut him off. "It's because it's not a curse."

The way the green thread was so tightly wound with the silver comes to mind. I bet if I looked again, it would be right back as to how it was before I touched it. I spread my palms on his furred chest and close my eyes to check. The world lights up in magic threads in my mind's eye and I laugh. Just as I thought, the green thread is back winding around the silver, as if they are making up a whole thread.

"How did you feel when I tried to untangle the curse?" I ask to make sure.

"Um, I'm not sure. I was feeling a lot of things." The gray of the skin of his cheekbones darkens in embarrassment. *Ah, because he'd just left me.* "But... drained, I guess. And a little nauseous."

I shake my head at both of our follies. If he'd only let me see him before...

"The logistics are unusual..." I trail off, thinking of the chances.

"Belinda." Jack shakes my hips a little to get my attention. "What are you saying?"

"Oh, sorry! You must have fae in you. Lycanthrope, I'd be willing to bet."

"What?"

"Hybrids don't usually happen," I say. "For most beings anyway."

I make a gesture in the air, not wanting to go into the way magics and genetics interact.

"There have been guesses that lycanthropes from the fae plane were the first wolf shifters, but that doesn't really make sense because the appearance isn't the same and the differences in anatomy," I say.

Jack shakes his head. "But I'm a wolf shifter. I had my first shift when I was twelve."

"That's the thing," I start. "Shifters shift with puberty. I bet if I do some research, we'll find that lycanthrope strength grows with age. You could have been dormant… until you weren't."

The longer Jack blinks at me, the surer I become.

Finally, he clears his throat. "What you're saying is that you think this is how I'm supposed to be?"

And this is how he'll stay.

I bite my lip before nodding. "Yeah. You can always see about being trained in fae magic instead of using a manufactured glamour by someone else."

I wait for Jack's reaction, knowing this isn't the answer he was looking for. This isn't anything in the realm of what he expected.

"Not a curse after all," Jack whispers, dropping his gaze to where he's gripping my hip.

"Are you okay?" I ask.

"Just processing. I've had so many hang-ups about being turned into a corrupted version of myself and you're telling me that I'm actually something else entirely."

I narrow my eyes at him. "I'm saying that you're just a different kind of monster and that there's nothing wrong with you."

The grip on my hips tightens as his eyes meet mine. "And you're a fan of monsters, aren't you?"

I rock my hips and grind against the cording of his stomach. "I seem to have a soft spot for them."

Jack smiles and the number of sharp teeth revealed startles me, but his mirth is tangible. "In your heart?"

My nose scrunches. "Well yes, but also somewhere lower."

He growls and sits up, his arms wrapping around me. "You're insatiable."

My teasing falls away. "Just with you. Do you think you'll be okay?"

"Yeah. I'm going to be better than okay." His nose brushes against mine. "Even if my entire world feels different, I have my mate by my side."

My joy overflows, and my smile widens. Fears that he'd run away from this, from me, again are dismissed by those words. Whatever there is to face, we'll face it together.

"Yes, you do," I say.

"And I'm glad that my mate is a fan of monsters."

That he can say *monster* without flinching when he's used it negatively for so long makes my heart sing, but that song stutters at the direct look in his gaze. The tension between us builds, and my pussy throbs at the sudden change, no matter the ache of soreness.

"I think my mate lusts for something else too," he muses.

"What?" I ask, my eyes big.

"To be chased."

A thrill shoots up my spine. "I can't be running in the woods barefoot and naked."

Jack's smile is part terrifying and part thrilling.

"Oh, you won't make it that far," he says.

My heartbeat thunders in my ears and the muscles of my legs tense. Jack's face comes near mine and the brush of his breath against my face adds to my adrenaline.

"Run," he commands.

I'm helpless to resist.

I shoot to my feet and dash away as a bone-chilling howl rises behind me.

EPILOGUE
JACK

"You don't have to do this," Bel says. She squeezes my human-appearing hand over the center console. It had taken a month of training with the lycanthrope we'd found, but now I can walk the world disguised in a glamour of my own making. I can appear human every moment for the rest of my life if I wish it.

But no matter what I look like, it doesn't change what I am, who I am.

And Bel would be disappointed if I never let my wilder side free.

No worry creases my mate's face, and her eyes are warm. She's confident in whatever I choose to do.

"I want to," I say.

"Good," she says with a crook of her lips. "Now help me with the food. We'll be late if we wait much longer."

I laugh and get out of the car with her. Nerves climb in my throat as I remove my clothing, leaving a pair of shorts that are a nod to decency if a ridiculous one. I take a deep breath, focusing on the magic running through my veins that I'd spent so long misinterpreting.

Before, it had been a tingling sensation, numbed by my purposeful avoidance. The strange feelings plaguing me after I'd reached fae maturity were just one more thing that felt *wrong*. Now, it's a bright sensation that I'm attuned to, and if I focus, can pick out the small flickers of fae magic that is intertwined in this plane.

I use the awareness to remove my glamour. The process is like casting off faint spiderwebs, and like the magic it is, the human form I'd had before is gone. I swallow down at my clawed feet.

"Jack," Belinda calls from the other side of the vehicle, in the tone that she uses when she's going to ask for something. Right. The food.

I take a deep breath, hearing easy conversations and the laughter of children nearby. The scent of cooking meat is in the air.

It's a beautiful day for a barbecue.

I round the car and Belinda loads me up with more side dishes than what we were instructed to bring, and I have a suspicion that it's her way of trying to put me at ease. Give the lycanthrope a task so he doesn't get too introspective. I've gotten to know my mate pretty well in the more than half a year we've been together. Just like she's gotten to know all my anxieties.

I smile at my mate. "I'm fine, Bel."

Her lips twitch and she gives me a once over. "You're more than fine."

Belinda blushes, and the surge of hunger the flush of her cheeks inspires is all the distraction I need. Our life together doesn't lack heated moments, but I find that no matter how many times I claim her, the burn of pleasure between us doesn't dim.

Mated life is bliss.

I take another deep breath and move toward the crowd of people.

"Jack!" Elliot Bramblewick is at the grill and wears an apron stating *Kiss the* Cook that looks ridiculous on the gargoyle.

I raise my hand in acknowledgment and let my eyes scan the crowd. Many are people I work with day to day, but there are also those who used to work at the company and were adopted into the embrace of the Bramblewick family. Everyone socializes warmly, with some keeping their eyes on the children running around.

There are more strangers than I've ever exposed my appearance to at once before, but the nerves lingering in my stomach dissipate quickly. There are many more nonhuman-appearing beings here than there are human looking. I've learned more about the beings that populate our world now that the mystery of my *curse* has been solved. I pick out the types of beings I can identify: an ogre, a few types of serpent kin, a variation of goblin, and of course, the Bramblewick gargoyles.

The Bramblewicks arranged for this picnic deep in wolf shifter territory so that everyone could be as open about their true nature as possible.

I'm not out of place. No one is staring at my fur or ears. The only response I get are the nods from people and greetings.

It's hard not to get choked up about it, but to everyone else here, this is a normal holiday picnic.

Belinda is on the move as soon as we set the food down, socializing from group to group like a butterfly. I follow her lead and make conversation until we come to people I recognize.

"This is quite the turnout," I say to Alasdair and Broderick Bramblewick while Belinda catches up with their witch mate, Grace.

The large gargoyle's eyes scan the crowd, and his smile is warm. "It is. I'm glad so many people could make it out this year."

One of the blanket bundles on his chest squirms and Alasdair adjusts the infant, but a whipcord gray tail lashes from the other blanket and he makes a sound of disappointment.

Broderick grins. "You can't just expect both of them to stay asleep on you the whole time, Alasdair."

Alasdair sighs. "They're just growing so fast. I don't want to miss a moment."

Broderick takes the fussier of the bundles, and the sleepier twin settles back down, his tiny tail slowing until it wraps around Alasdair's wrist in an adorable way.

A stab of yearning sharpens in me as Broderick makes funny faces at his son. The Bramblewicks never turn down an opportunity to show off their young, and I don't blame them.

Belinda and I have discussed kids in a distant way. We want them but haven't said when.

While I worked to adjust to the reality of being a lycanthrope, everything else was put on hold. Now, my mentor is impressed with how I'm adapting to my inner beast. I don't tell him that I've promised to give my "wolf" what he wants. It's easier to manage him when he knows that our mate will end up bred by us eventually.

Excitement sparks at the thought. Maybe Bel and I should revisit the topic.

***

ᴄBELINDA

"Do you want to hold him?" Grace asks, and I realize I've been staring.

Broderick had to leave the picnic table to help Elliot with the food, and Grace had taken her infant from her mate with gusto. The baby has settled now but is very awake. The small clawed hands grab at Grace's fingers as she entertains her son.

A gray fist curls tight before the baby stuffs it in his mouth, and I laugh. He's such a character.

I start to say no but stop. He's really cute. I'm sure just holding him for a minute wouldn't make me want things that I've determined to be patient about more than I already do.

"I think I would," I say.

Grace smiles as if she understands how taken I am with her baby. She probably does.

"Make sure to keep his wings next to his body. They're small right now, but flexible."

She places the warm weight in my arms, and he wiggles. I smile at him, and he stops wiggling. He blinks at me before smiling back, all gums save for two tiny fangs.

"Aw, look at that. Lachlan's found a new best friend," Grace coos.

"He's adorable," I say.

"And a troublemaker already. I can't wait to see what kind of destruction he and his brother Graham will get into. At least the delight of having three mates is that there are more than enough hands to go around."

"I bet." I bite my lip. I don't need three mates, but baby Lachlan is definitely giving me baby fever. Instead of a little gray face with curled horns nestled in fluffy black hair, I'm thinking of a baby that would be a mix of Jack and my features.

Maybe the lycanthrope blood would show true at the beginning, but most likely, our child would start as a wolf shifter. Witches don't usually produce witches when we mix with nonhumans. I'm getting ahead of myself. Jack might want to wait longer.

Lachlan's little tail wraps around my wrist and my heart melts.

I look up to check on my mate and freeze. Jack stares at me with a look hot enough to scorch. It's almost uncomfortable to hold Lachlan with how my body instantly responds, so I look away.

My smile is slow, but wide. At least I have company in my baby fever.

***

"There's a nature walk that the Bramblewicks thought we might like." Jack makes a turn instead of heading the way we came. He's back in his glamour so he can drive, but I can still read the sexual frustration in his posture and the tightness of his jaw. The hours it had been for the picnic to wind down were low-key torture with the thoughts swirling in my mind.

I'll bet there is a beautiful nature walk, and I'll bet it's private. It would seem Grace is looking to acquire a playmate for her sons, and I don't mind the interference a bit.

"That's the marker." Jack parks the car beside a trailhead, well away from the dying embers of the party, but neither of us moves to get out.

"Soooo, did you want to talk about something?" I tease.

Jack raises a brow. "Did you?"

He tries to play it cool, but I see the way his eyes rove over me and if he grips the steering wheel any harder, it's going to break. I take mercy on him, mostly because I want to hurry this along. I'm so wet, it's a surprise that I'm not making a mess in the passenger seat.

Jack will definitely make a mess of me.

"I want to have babies with you," I say, my breath catching as I outpace my nerves. "And if you're ready to have babies with me…" I trail off and drag my contraceptive charm back and forth on its chain.

"I want that too," he says. "I want it so much. I want to breed you," Jack's voice growls and he clears his throat, clearly struggling to keep his wolf from taking over.

I swallow, my skin on fire now.

The chain around my neck snaps and I look down at the delicate thing that's kept me from getting pregnant up until this point.

"Oops," I say.

Fate is at it again, or I don't know my own strength when I want my mate to fill me up. I drop the charm and it falls to be forever lost in the crack between the seat belt and center console. The drag of the chain on my skin as it goes has me biting my lip. Everything is unbearably sensitive. My sundress feels two sizes too small, and my breasts seem like they're fighting to get free.

"Bel…" Jack says, clearly losing control because my name is all growl now.

I swallow, my chest rising and falling quickly in the tense atmosphere of the car. The forest outside calls to me, an echo of the first time we came together with the full moon bright. I know exactly how I want this to happen.

"You'll be a good dad," I say before giving him a naughty smile. "But you'll have to catch me first."

I jump out of the car and run as fast as I can. The snarl from the car is a deeper, more primal sound than I've ever heard from my mate, but I don't hesitate.

The night air is cold, leaves and twigs smack and scratch me, but I hardly feel it. I'm high on the chase, only focusing on the fire building in my body and the path in front of me. My lungs burn and I try to push past it. This isn't like the other times we've played a game of chase. This has stakes. Compulsively I want to make Jack work for this, fight to breed me.

Oh my gods. I almost trip. The thought of that is enough to kick the throb between my legs even higher.

I don't hear him pursuing me, but I don't dare stop running to check. I dodge trees and wind through branches. The moonlight is bright and makes it easier to see the ground.

Just when I'm wondering why Jack is letting me get so far, he strikes.

A body collides with mine, and we both go sprawling on the moss-covered ground. Instead of laughing and submitting to my mate how I normally would, I struggle. Instincts that I hardly recognize are screaming at me to make Jack earn the right to fuck his baby into me.

I thrash against him, using my legs and arms to try and move his large body and escape. The ground scrapes against my skin and heightens the sensation.

A contrary battle takes place inside me. I throb, achy and so wet my inner thighs and pussy are soaked under my sundress, but I don't give in. The struggle is honest.

Luckily for both our bodies, Jack is much stronger than I am. I end up on my hands and knees, his hand gripping the back of my neck.

"MINE!" he bellows. The timbre of the word hits me low in my belly, and sharp teeth press against my mating mark.

I cry out in relief as the fight leaves me. I stop struggling, and the tantalizing teeth disappear with a deep sound of approval. I groan, subdued and needy. My dress is pushed up without preamble, and I sink my chest lower to the ground, knowing what comes next from all the times we've done this before.

The action has never felt this tense, and I've never felt as absolutely desperate to experience the stretch of him inside me as I do now. Distantly I wonder if lycanthropes can throw their mate into a heat-like experience because I've never been so turned on and so wanting to be filled until his seed leaks from me.

My wet underwear rips as if they're paper, the fabric digging into my hip, and the stab of pain just makes me hotter.

"My mate," Jack growls, his claws gripping my hips firmly.

I moan. "Yes."

"You're so wet for me. I could scent you wherever you'd run in this forest." His grip tightens and I pant.

My keyed-up body tenses around nothing.

"You're mine. I've fought and claimed you under this moon. I'll fill your womb until you carry my young."

YES! I almost can't breathe from the desire pounding in my heart.

I whimper in relief when I hear the slick slide of Jack's cock unsheathing and his wet thickness slides down my ass. I move my hips back against the probing tip of him. Its wetness mixing with my own.

I know what's coming, but it still surprises me.

Jack thrusts into me without warning, and I grunt.

"Oh fuck," I whine, losing control of my body for a moment, thrashing, fighting his forging thickness. But it's a useless fight. He dominates me, filling me up until I can only receive *him*.

My body adjusts like it always does, and my struggle ceases as I groan at the heavy feel of him inside me, knowing each slide will eventually lead him to spill his seed into me and being needy for it.

"More," I slur, lust drunk.

My mate gives me what I'm asking for, working his cock deeper and deeper inside me. Each thrust of his hips has him grunting.

"So tight. You fit me perfectly."

His hips hit my ass, bottoming out the ridiculous size of him inside me, and I clench on it hungrily, letting out a desperate sound.

Everything is so much. Each slide of him and the thought of being owned so completely—bred—short-circuits my brain.

"Please, Jack, give it to me."

The thrusts are quick now, rutting. Each one hits me just right. The impacts send my mind spiraling in pleasure, higher and higher until I can't take it anymore.

"Take all my seed, mate. I want you round and growing with what I give you," he growls.

"Yes!" I shout.

His knot swells and the internal locking pressure kicks off my release. I cry out as Jack howls in victory, spilling himself deep, heating me from the inside. His cum fills me up, overfull and stretching for him. We both groan when his cock throbs again, spilling even more into me.

It takes minutes, but eventually both of our breaths slow and I notice more things other than the knot stretching me. The light breeze and sound of crickets. The earthy scent of the disturbed ground and moss under us. I was right. Jack made a mess of me. My hands and knees are surely stained with green and dirt.

Jack nuzzles and lifts me up, careful of where we are still connected. He lies down against a tree and I lie back against him. He nibbles on my mating mark, and I sigh in pleasure. We stay like that until the knot slides free from me.

I turn in his arms without hesitation, straddling his front. My fingers comb through the ruff of fur at his neck and wander over him, his snout, and ears. Jack relaxes under the soft touches.

I rest my forehead to his and whisper. "I love you, my monster."

"And I love you, my feisty mate." Jack's grip tightens on me and he presses his hips up against my sopping pussy. The throb of hardness as he starts to unsheathe catches me by surprise.

"Again?" I ask, breathless.

"I made an oath under the full moon." Jack's words are teasing. "It would be bad luck not to fulfill it."

I'll fill your womb until you carry my young.

"*Oh gods*," I say, even as excitement intertwines with arousal again. "We wouldn't dare break an oath like that."

Jack's chuckle is dark, and my monster fulfills every oath he's ever made.

THE END

Note From the Author

Hello Dear Reader!

Thank you for reading Ensnared by the Werewolf!

An early version of the story was included in my very first anthology and more than a few readers requested it as a separate book. Which was convenient because I wanted to release it as such. It was a blast to delve back into this story to add Jack's perspective and how mated life looks for this couple.

A thank you to Liz Alden for beta reading this rejected mate tale. Your insights help me fill in all the holes... in the plot.

As always, thank you, Dear Reader, for reading my book. It's always a marvelous thing that people read the books that I create and I'm grateful to you.

About the Author

Lillian Lark was born and raised in the saltiest of cities in Utah. Lillian is an avid reader, cat mom to three demons, and loves writing sexy stories that twist you up inside.

More information about Lillian can be found on her website at LillianLark.com